P9-DWO-119

Dear Parents and Educators,

Welcome to Penguin Young Readers! As parents and educators, you know that each child develops at his or her own pace—in terms of speech, critical thinking, and, of course, reading. Penguin Young Readers recognizes this fact. As a result, each Penguin Young Readers book is assigned a traditional easy-to-read level (1–4) as well as a Guided Reading Level (A–P). Both of these systems will help you choose the right book for your child. Please refer to the back of each book for specific leveling information. Penguin Young Readers features esteemed authors and illustrators, stories about favorite characters, fascinating nonfiction, and more!

Tiny Goes to the Movies

LEVEL **2**

GUIDED
READING
LEVEL **E**

This book is perfect for a **Progressing Reader** who:
• can figure out unknown words by using picture and context clues;
• can recognize beginning, middle, and ending sounds;
• can make and confirm predictions about what will happen in the text;and
• can distinguish between fiction and nonfiction.

Here are some **activities** you can do during and after reading this book:
• Make Connections: In the story, Tiny and his best friend bring popcorn, a blanket, and a chair to the movie night in the park. If you were going to a movie night, what would you bring?
• Make Predictions: Tiny and his best friend love swimming and playing ball in the summer. What do you think they will do together in the fall?

Remember, sharing the love of reading with a child is the best gift you can give!

—Bonnie Bader, EdM
  Penguin Young Readers program

*Penguin Young Readers are leveled by independent reviewers applying the standards developed by Irene Fountas and Gay Su Pinnell in *Matching Books to Readers: Using Leveled Books in Guided Reading*, Heinemann, 1999.

For Jameson—CM

To all the kids through the years in Club 56
who have spent time in our home learning to
love and follow Jesus . . . I am proud of you
and look forward to watching you continue to
grow and be world-changers. I love you—RD

PENGUIN YOUNG READERS
An Imprint of Penguin Random House LLC

Library of Congress Cataloging-in-Publication Data is available.

ISBN 978-0-448-48295-8 (pbk)   10 9 8 7 6 5 4 3 2 1
ISBN 978-0-448-48296-5 (hc)   10 9 8 7 6 5 4 3 2 1

PENGUIN YOUNG READERS

LEVEL 2
PROGRESSING READER

TiNY Goes to the Movies

by Cari Meister
illustrated by Rich Davis

Penguin Young Readers
An Imprint of Penguin Random House

I love summer.

So does Tiny.

We like to swim.

We like to play ball.

We like to watch movies.

Tonight is movie night

at the park.

I pop popcorn.

Oh no! Too much popcorn!

It is okay.

Tiny cleans up.

Time to go!

I bring the popcorn.

Tiny brings a blanket

and a chair.

We find a good spot.

Tiny is too big.

We have to move.

That is okay.

This spot is better.

Soon it is dark.

Tiny is scared.

I rub his ears.

It is okay, Tiny.

I am here.

The movie starts.

A cat comes on the screen.

Tiny barks.

Tiny barks and barks.

22

No, Tiny! No barking.

3

Tiny runs at the cat.

He runs and runs.

Stop, Tiny!

Oh no!

Tiny makes a mess.

He tries to clean up.

They say no.

We go home.

It is okay, Tiny.

We can watch a movie

at home!